♥ Mindy Kim and the
Trip to Korea ♥

Don't miss more fun adventures
with **Mindy Kim**!

# Mindy Kim

### and the
## Trip to Korea

BOOK
**5**

By Lyla Lee
Illustrated by Dung Ho

**ALADDIN**
New York  London  Toronto  Sydney  New Delhi

ALADDIN
An imprint of Simon & Schuster Children's Publishing Division
1230 Avenue of the Americas, New York, New York 10020
First Aladdin hardcover edition June 2021
Text copyright © 2021 by Lyla Lee
Illustrations copyright © 2021 by Dung Ho
Also available in an Aladdin paperback edition.
All rights reserved, including the right of reproduction in whole or in part in any form.
ALADDIN and related logo are registered trademarks of Simon & Schuster, Inc.
For information about special discounts for bulk purchases, please contact Simon & Schuster Special Sales at 1-866-506-1949 or business@simonandschuster.com.
The Simon & Schuster Speakers Bureau can bring authors to your live event. For more information or to book an event contact the Simon & Schuster Speakers Bureau at 1-866-248-3049 or visit our website at www.simonspeakers.com.
Designed by Laura Lyn DiSiena
The illustrations for this book were rendered digitally.
The text of this book was set in Haboro.
Manufactured in the United States of America 0421 FFG
10 9 8 7 6 5 4 3 2 1
This book has been cataloged with the Library of Congress.
ISBN 978-1-5344-8895-3 (hc)
ISBN 978-1-5344-8894-6 (pbk)
ISBN 978-1-5344-8896-0 (eBook)

To my grandparents. 사랑해요.

# Chapter 1

My name is Mindy Kim. I am nine years old, and today I'm going to Korea for the first time ever!

My mom and dad were born in South Korea, but I was born in San Francisco. So my parents have been to Korea lots of times but not me. I've only been to California and Florida and that's it. I'm so nervous about my first trip out of the country!

"Psst, are you up, Mindy?"

Dad peeked into my room, and a sliver of light from the hallway lit up my bed. It was still dark outside, but we had to get up really early to catch our flight.

The truth was, I hadn't slept one bit. I was way too excited! But I didn't want Dad to worry. So I slowly got out of my bed with a big yawn like I was just waking up.

"Yup!" I said. "Ready to go, Appa."

*Appa* means "Daddy" in Korean. Sometimes I call him Dad and sometimes I call him Appa.

Dad smiled. "Good! I'll meet you downstairs. Is your suitcase ready?"

I nodded and rolled it over to Dad so he could carry it down the stairs. My suitcase was super cute, with pink hearts and a cute cat on the front. Dad had bought it for me last week so I could pack for this trip.

I wasn't an expert on what to pack for Korea, but luckily, Dad was. He helped me pack my suitcase in no time! The only thing I really wanted to bring was my dog, Theodore the Mutt. But Dad said it would be too stressful for Theodore.

"A lot of dogs don't handle flying on planes well," he'd explained. "And it's too short a trip for him to get used to everything. That's why we're leaving him with Mrs. Park and Eunice–it's for the best!"

Eunice is my babysitter, but this summer, she was going to be Theodore's. Eunice is the best babysitter ever!

We dropped Theodore off at Eunice's house last night. He looked so confused and whined a lot when Dad and I left. It made me really sad, but I knew this was for his own good. Plus, he could play with Eunice's dog, Oliver the Maltese! Theodore and Oliver are best friends. Even though I was super excited to go on my first trip to Korea, I already missed Theodore. I hoped he'd have tons of fun with Oliver!

"Mindy! Are you ready?" Dad called from downstairs. "We need to head out!"

"Coming!" I yelled.

I looked around my room one last time before heading toward the door. Usually it's messy because Theodore and I like to play a lot. But last night, I'd cleaned my room after we dropped Theodore off. So everything was super clean. It looked like someone else's room!

"Good-bye, room," I whispered. "See you in two weeks!"

My room didn't say anything back, but it looked empty and lonely without Theodore and me. I took a deep breath and closed the door.

Dad and I picked up Julie on our way to the airport. Julie is Dad's girlfriend, and it was her first time going to Korea too! She was coming with us to meet my dad's family. My best friend Sally said that this was a sign that things were "getting serious" between her and Dad.

"It's just like in the movies I watch with my mom!" she had said when I called her last week. "Soon they'll get married and live happily ever after!"

I wasn't sure what she meant by "happily ever after." Dad and Mom had gotten married, but then Mom had gotten sick. I hoped Julie wouldn't get sick too.

After she loaded her suitcase into the trunk, Julie got into the back seat so she could sit with me. She looked a little pale and sweaty.

"Are you okay?" I asked her. "You look sick!"

Julie nodded. "I'm just nervous about meeting your family. I hope they like me!"

"Don't worry, Julie–my grandma and grandpa are really nice!"

Even though this was my first time going to Korea, my grandparents had visited us a lot back when Dad and I lived in California. Whenever they came, they brought me tons of cute stuff, like Mrs. Poodle and Mr. Toe Beans, two of my stuffed animals.

Dad glanced back at us from the front seat. "Yeah, I'm sure my parents will love you, Julie. You even learned Korean so you could talk with them!"

Julie and I had spent the last few months practicing Korean together for the trip. My Korean was okay, enough to talk to my grandparents on the phone. But ever since Mom died, I hadn't used

Korean much, so I was really rusty. The good news was, I could still say all the important things, like "Thank you!" and "Where is the bathroom?"

Julie smiled. "Let's hope so. Are you excited about the trip, Mindy?"

"Yup, it's my first trip to another country! Dad helped me set up a blog so I can write about our trip. I'm going to take lots of pictures!"

"Oh, wow, how cool! I'll be sure to check out your blog. You must be so excited! I had so many butterflies in my stomach when I traveled to another country for the first time. I went to China to visit my family, just like you're going to Korea to visit yours!"

When we arrived at the airport, there were lots of people lined up to check their bags in already. I was so glad that we left the house early!

The line moved really slowly, like a snail, so I got bored and looked around. People around us talked in different languages. Behind us, two kids with travel pillows were fighting in Spanish, and in front of us, a group of high school kids chatted in Chinese. We were all headed for big adventures!

There weren't any direct flights from Orlando, so we had to fly to Atlanta before going to Korea. The flight to Atlanta was pretty boring, and it was only an hour and a half long. I couldn't even finish one movie!

"We still have a few hours before our next flight," Dad said when we got off our plane. "Let's stretch our legs a bit and get something to eat. Remember, we'll be cooped up in the plane for fourteen and a half hours!"

"Fourteen and a half hours!" Even though Dad had already told me how long the flight was, I still couldn't imagine being in the plane for so long. The flight from California to Florida had been only around five hours, and that had seemed like forever. I hoped I wouldn't get bored.

When we reached our next terminal, I peered out the window. Our plane to Korea looked really different from the one we'd taken to Atlanta. It was a lot larger and a pretty sky-blue color!

We still had a lot of time left, so after eating an early lunch, Dad, Julie, and I began stretching. Dad isn't very flexible, so he made lots of funny faces and noises while touching his toes and stretching his arms. People turned around to stare at us, and Julie and I giggled. Dad was so funny!

And then it was finally time for us to board our plane to Korea. I was so excited!

*Korea, here I come!*

# Chapter 2

The flight to Korea was *really* long. I slept, watched three movies about dogs, and played Pokémon on my Nintendo Switch. Julie read a book, and Dad slept for almost the entire flight. He was snoring so loudly that the lady in front of us kept glaring at us!

The best thing about the flight was the food. For all our meals, the flight attendants gave us a choice of either Korean food or Western food. I got bulgogi for one meal, bibimbap for another, and an omelet for the last one!

During our flight, I also kept track of where our plane was on the map. It was really cool to see our plane fly across the ocean. We were traveling such a long way! I especially liked it when the words on the map switched from English to Korean to Chinese. I wasn't very good at reading or writing Korean, but I liked how I could sound out a lot of the place names in Korean by using the English names.

After what seemed like forever, we finally touched down! We went through customs and grabbed our bags. Dad called my uncle, who was picking us up with my cousins. I was super excited to meet them, but I was super nervous, too. I hoped they'd like me!

Dad told me that my cousins learned English in school, but they didn't know a lot of words. I hoped they could teach me more Korean and I could help them with English!

While Dad was trying to reach my uncle, I scanned the crowd of faces. And then I saw them. My uncle and my cousins!

"Appa, look! They're over there!"

I'd never seen my uncle and cousins in person before, but I recognized them from pictures and our video chats. They were waving at us with big

grins on their faces and were holding a big sign with cute pink letters that said *Welcome, Mindy! Welcome, Julie!* The sign also had a picture of an adorable dog. They knew me so well already!

Dad and my uncle hugged, greeting each other in Korean. Julie bowed and greeted him with "Ahnyeonghaseyo!" It's how you say hi in a very polite way in Korean.

"Min-jung," my uncle said, calling me by my Korean name. "Welcome to Korea!"

"Thanks, Keun Appa!" I said. "It's nice to finally meet you in person!"

In Korea, people don't just say "Uncle" and "Aunt" like we do in America. Instead you use different words for uncles or aunts, depending on how they're related to your parents! Since this uncle is Dad's big brother, I'm supposed to call him Keun Appa and call his wife Keun Umma.

I looked around to greet my cousins. On Dad's side, I have two cousins, Sora and Sung-jin. Their last name is Kim, like mine! Sora is three years younger than me while Sung-jin is a year older.

Sung-jin gave me a hug, but Sora was nowhere in sight. *Where did she go?*

"Sorry," Keun Appa said. "Sora's hiding behind me. She's really shy."

I still remembered what it was like to be six. I was a lot shyer back then too.

"Hi, Sora," I said in a quiet voice. I tried giving her my most friendly smile. "I'm Mindy, but my Korean name is Min-jung. It's nice to meet you!"

Sora smiled, just a tiny bit, but she stayed behind Keun Appa.

"It's okay," Keun Appa said. "She'll warm up to you soon."

Dad and Keun Appa got the bags, and then we all walked out of the airport. Outside was super busy, with people talking in Korean. Everyone was speaking really fast, so I couldn't catch a lot of what they were saying, but I understood some words, like "five" and "car."

When we got to the van, Sung-jin crawled in first to sit in the third row by himself. He was busy playing games on his phone, so he didn't seem to mind. Dad sat with Keun Appa in the front, while Julie, Sora, and I sat in the second row.

My family lives about three hours away from the airport, but the drive seemed a lot longer. In the beginning, Keun Appa asked me questions like "How was your flight?" and "What do you want to do in Korea?" But then the adults talked by themselves and left me out! It was mostly Dad and Keun Appa speaking in Korean, while Julie smiled and nodded when they talked to her in English. I guess they had a lot to catch up on.

After a while, I got bored and tried chatting with my cousins. But Sung-jin was still busy with his game, while Sora just stared at me with wide eyes. I don't think she understood a lot of what I said in English.

I thought about switching to Korean, but then I wasn't sure what we could talk about. I was way better at speaking English than Korean. And I didn't know what Sora would want to talk about, period. She and I were almost complete strangers!

I thought very hard about what I'd liked when

I was six. But then I remembered the dog on the welcome sign. I'd loved dogs my whole life. Maybe Sora liked dogs too!

"Dad?" I said. "Can I borrow your tablet?"

"Sure!" He fished the tablet out of his backpack and passed it back to me.

I pulled up pictures of Theodore and showed it to Sora.

"This is my dog," I said in Korean. "His name is Theodore the Mutt! Do you like dogs?"

Sora's face lit up. Even Sung-jin paused his game so he could look at Theodore!

"We have a dog too!" she replied. "Her name is Danbi."

Sung-jin closed the game on his phone to show me a picture of their dog, a cute little yellow Pomeranian. She was so fluffy!

"She's so cute!" I exclaimed. "I can't wait to meet her!"

For the rest of the car ride, my cousins and I talked about dogs, using both Korean and English. Dog loving clearly ran in the family!

# Chapter 3

Korea is so different from Florida. There aren't any palm trees, but there are mountains like in California. But unlike California, there are a lot more people and apartments, too!

The Korean apartment buildings are way taller than the apartment buildings back home. They are skinnier, and some even towered more than thirty floors above us as we made our way into the city. I'd never seen apartment buildings so tall before. They're almost skyscrapers!

When we got to my family's town, we passed by an apartment that had a really tall ladder with a lift propped up against its side. From way, way up high, movers loaded a piano onto the lift and lowered it down to a truck below.

"That's how Korean people move out of their homes, Mindy!" Dad explained. "It's so different from how we moved, right?"

"Yeah!" I replied. "It's so cool!"

When we moved to Florida, the movers carried our stuff into our house because it was only two stories tall. We definitely didn't need a tall lift to move our things!

"We're almost home," Keun Appa announced. "Just five minutes."

We all cheered. I was hungry and sleepy. I couldn't wait to eat Grandma's cooking again. She is the best cook in the entire universe! And I was so excited to see my grandparents in person again.

When we finally arrived, my aunt and my grandparents greeted me with open arms in the first-floor lobby.

"Min-jung!" Grandma said in Korean. "You've gotten so tall!"

She gave me a great big hug. Grandma smelled really nice, like freshly made steamed buns.

"How was your flight?" Grandpa asked when he hugged me next.

"It was great! They gave us lots of yummy food!"

Grandpa laughed. "Well, I hope you saved room for dinner, because Grandma prepared a lot of food for you!"

"I always have room for Grandma's cooking!" I declared.

Everyone laughed.

"It's so nice to finally meet you in person, Min-jung!" my aunt said.

"It's so nice to meet you too, Keun Umma!" I said.

Julie said hi to everyone too, going around to shake hands. When she reached Grandma, though, Grandma just grinned tightly, like she'd eaten something funny. Grandpa also looked pretty awkward. I guess they were feeling shy about meeting Dad's girlfriend.

Julie looked really sad. I hoped my grandparents would warm up to her soon!

When we went up to my family's apartment on the twenty-sixth floor, Danbi the Pomeranian started barking really loudly before we even opened the door.

"She's friendly," Keun Appa assured us. "She just barks a lot."

He opened the door and Danbi shot out like a rocket! She jumped up and down, trying to lick my face.

"Hi, Danbi!" I said. "It's nice to meet you! You're so cute!"

I tried petting her soft, poofy fur, but she wiggled around too much. She was way more hyper than Theodore!

Dad and Keun Appa dragged our suitcases in first, and we all followed them inside. The entire apartment smelled like freshly cooked bulgogi, steamed buns, and Korean pancakes. My mouth started watering!

My jaw dropped when I saw the kitchen table. From one edge to another, the table was covered with almost every kind of Korean food I knew,

including seafood pancakes, four different types of kimchi, and galbi ribs. It was a grand feast!

"Wow," I said. "The food looks like it could be on TV!"

Everyone laughed. I heard my grandparents say, "Gwiyeowo," which means "cute" in Korean.

The food was as good as it looked. If I could eat Grandma's cooking forever, I would!

During dinner, everyone asked me questions in both Korean and English.

"Mindy, how is school in America?"

"Do you have any friends? What are their names?"

"How old is your dog?"

I tried my best to answer all the questions, but after a while, I became dizzy. Switching between languages was tough, and I couldn't understand some of the Korean questions!

Back at home, it was usually just Dad and me eating dinner together. It was nice to have a big family, but I wished I'd studied more Korean so I could understand more of what everyone was say-

llo?" she said. "Is that you, Mindy? Why are
ing in the dark? How's Korea?"

a whole day in Korea, hearing just English
ttle weird. But seeing Sally's face cheered
lot!

four a.m. here!" I whispered, trying my best
my voice quiet. "We're thirteen whole hours
f you."

, cool! You're calling from the future!"
laimed. "How is it over there?"

led. "Korea is good! My grandma made
od food, the best food I've ever eaten in
life! But I can't understand a lot of what's
And I miss you and Theodore."

have sounded sad, because Sally frowned.
are you coming back?"

weeks. But I miss home already."

kind of like how I was when my family
urope last summer. I was super lonely
nd when we went to Spain and France,
nderstand what people were saying, so
confusing. But it was still a good trip.

ing. Dad translated for me when I didn't understand, but it wasn't the same.

Julie looked flustered too. My family asked her even *more* questions than they asked me!

By the time dinner was over, I was super sleepy and had a big headache.

"You look so tired, Mindy!" Dad said. "You're probably jet-lagged, and it's getting pretty late anyway. I'll ask Keun Appa to lay out the blankets."

Since the apartment only had three bedrooms, Dad, Julie, and I had to sleep on the blankets in the living room. In Korea, lots of people sleep on the floor, so this wasn't weird at all!

Keun Appa set up the blankets in the living room. The blankets were super thick and soft so people could lie on them to sleep. But I wished they were a little comfier. I missed my bed back home.

Even though I was happy to be in Korea, I felt sick and tired. I hoped I would feel better tomorrow.

# Chapter 4

The next morning when I opened my eyes, it was still dark outside. I checked the clock on the wall. It was four a.m.!

Julie and Dad were still fast asleep. Dad was snoring really loudly. He sounded like a lawn mower.

I squeezed my eyes shut and counted sheep. I breathed in and out really slowly. I even tried to read a book, but that didn't work at all. It was too dark to read without a light! I checked the clock again. It was only 4:10. Just ten minutes had passed since I woke up!

Dad had warned me about jet lag back when

we were getting ready for o
since Korea was on the oth
from Florida, it'd be nighttim
there. It had sounded cool v
it, but now it didn't feel that

Then I got an idea. I sc
can I use your tablet? I can

Dad woke up for a br
Mindy. Go ahead."

And then he was fast
lucky! I wished I could sle

I got Dad's iPad from
out to the patio.

Dad's tablet showec
and Florida. Even thou
Florida it was currently
wide awake!

I slid the glass d
wouldn't wake up any
Sally, my best friend.

She picked up aln

"He
you sit

Afte
felt a li
me up a

"It's
to keep
ahead o

"Wov
Sally exc

I smi
really go
my entire
going on.

I must
"Aw, when

"In two

"That's
went to F
then too. A
I couldn't u
it got reall

I bet you're gonna have lots of fun in Korea too! You're just not used to everything yet."

"Do you really think so?"

"Yup. Send me lots of pictures! I heard Korea is really pretty."

"Okay!"

I then told Sally all about my flight and how cool Korea was. I also told her about what my grandparents were like when they met Julie.

"Uh-oh," Sally said. "Do you think they don't like her?"

I frowned. "I don't know. They *really* liked my mom, so maybe they still feel awkward about everything."

"I guess that's understandable," Sally said. "Maybe they just need some time!"

After we hung up, I made the first post on my blog. Dad said I should write on the blog like I would talk to a friend, so I wrote like I was talking to Sally! Writing about my flight and my family made me feel a bit better.

When I finished, I turned off Dad's tablet and got back under my blanket. Dad was still snoring, but he was facing the other way now, so it wasn't so bad.

I closed my eyes and hoped Sally was right.

# Chapter 5

When I opened my eyes again, it was so bright outside!

"It's about time you woke up, Mindy!" Dad said with a laugh. "It's past noon!"

I looked out the window. The sun was high in the sky.

I was alone on the living room floor. Everyone else was eating lunch at the dining room table. The smell of food made my mouth water. I didn't feel sick anymore, and I was hungry again!

"You woke up just in time for lunch!" Grandma said. "Come sit at the table, Min-jung!"

I sat next to Dad. Keun Umma and Julie were

at the table too, but my uncle and my cousins were nowhere in sight.

"Where's Keun Appa?" I asked. "And Sora and Sung-jin?"

"Keun Appa went to work," Dad explained. "And your cousins are at school. In Korea, the school year is different from America, so kids have a short break in the summer and a longer one in the winter. You should play with them after they're back! We're not really doing anything today since everyone still needs to rest."

"Okay!" I said.

Lunch was mul naeng-myeon, yummy cold noodles that were perfect on a hot summer day like today. Grandma made her naeng-myeon all fancy with an egg, beef, and cucumbers. When Dad made naeng-myeon, it was just noodles and cucumbers!

I told Grandma this, and everyone laughed.

Dad blushed. "I'm usually too tired after work to make it with all the ingredients," he explained.

"It's okay," Grandma said. "Your dad works hard every day to take care of you."

"Yup!" I agreed. "Dad is doing his best. He's a good dad!"

Dad smiled. "Thanks, Mindy."

After lunch, Grandma and Keun Umma went out to get groceries while Dad took an afternoon nap. I guess he was jet-lagged too! Julie, though, didn't sleep. Instead she looked up stuff on her laptop with a frown on her face.

I finished a new blog entry–this one was about how good my grandma's cooking was!–and asked Julie, "Is everything okay?"

She glanced up from the computer and smiled at me, but she still looked worried. "Oh hi, Mindy. Everything's fine. I'm just having a hard time deciding something."

"Can I help?"

I plopped down next to her on the sofa and peered closely at her computer screen. She was looking at different types of Korean food!

Julie's face lit up. "Actually, yes!" she exclaimed. "Thanks for asking, Mindy! I'm trying to decide what food to make your family. I feel bad that your grandma and aunt are doing all the cooking. I figured it'd be a nice surprise if I made them food. Which of these is the yummiest?"

"Which of these is the yummiest?" is one of my favorite questions in the universe! I looked at the Korean food Julie had up on her screen. Even though I was full from lunch, the pictures looked so good that I felt hungry again.

"I really like kimbap!" I said. "My mom used to make it all the time. Japchae is really good too. They're the stir-fried glass noodles we had on Lunar New Year!"

"Ooh, I remember them!" Julie said. "Okay, I think I'll try my hand at kimbap first. Your dad told me we're all going up to Seoul tomorrow, but I can make it the day after!"

Seoul is the capital city of Korea. I'd only seen it in Korean TV shows, so I was really excited to see it in real life for myself!

"Okay!" I said. "Good luck with the cooking!"

I really liked Julie, so I hoped my grandparents would like her too. Hopefully, the kimbap would help! My mom used to always say that the best way to people's hearts was their stomach.

For the rest of the day, I read. Before we left on our trip, Dad had bought me a guidebook about Korea. It was really helpful, and I was learning so much about my culture!

When my cousins came home from school, I felt shy. I wanted to play with them, but I had no idea what kids in Korea liked to do! I only knew that my cousins liked dogs.

In the end, I chickened out and played with Danbi the Pomeranian instead. Dogs were so much easier to be friends with than people!

Dad found me playing with Danbi on the patio and frowned. "Mindy, your cousins are back from school. Why don't you go play with them in their room?"

I looked at the floor. "Okay, I'll try."

When I got there, though, I heard familiar video game sounds coming from the room. I'd recognize the ding-ding-dings and the happy music any-where. It was *Mario Kart*!

My friends from school like playing *Mario Kart* too. We play it all the time during birthday parties.

I opened the door and said, "Can I play too?"

Sung-jin looked up from the TV. He was racing as Yoshi while Sora was racing as Wario!

"Sure!" he said. "You can join in the next race."

Sora and Sung-jin entered the last lap, and I cheered for both of them. In the end, Sora won, beating Sung-jin by three whole places!

"Way to go!" I gave her a high five.

"Thanks!" She beamed.

"I'll for sure win next time," Sung-jin said. "Grab a controller and join, Min-jung!"

Soon we were playing and laughing all afternoon. Even though I couldn't understand a lot of what they said, I had so much fun!

# Chapter

# 6

On Friday, Dad rented a car and the entire family left for Seoul! My grandparents rode with Dad, Julie, and me, while my cousins' family took their car. Keun Appa took the day off from work and my cousins took the day off school just so they could spend time with us! I felt really special.

It was a two-and-a-half-hour drive from my family's town to Seoul. At the beginning of the car ride, Julie, Dad, and I talked a lot in English. But then Dad talked to my grandparents in really fast Korean, so Julie and I were left out! Dad tried to loop us back in, translating when he could. When we entered the city, though, Dad focused on driving, so everyone was quiet.

In the capital city, there were so many cars, and everyone was honking. It reminded me of when my parents and I went to San Francisco! San Francisco is a busy city too.

The first place we were going to go was the Namdaemun Market. It's the largest market in all of Korea!

"Just pick whatever you want, Mindy. Harabeoji will buy everything for you," Grandpa said. *Harabeoji* is the Korean word for "grandpa."

"That won't be necessary," Dad said. "I can buy things for her myself."

Grandpa laughed. "You can't blame an old man for wanting to get his granddaughter souvenirs so she can remember her trip. It's okay! I buy gifts for Sora and Sung-jin all the time. Right, kids?"

Sora and Sung-jin grinned.

"I manage to pay for most of them at the last minute, though," Keun Appa said quietly, so Grandpa couldn't hear him. "But he's a real fighter. Best of luck trying to convince him to not pay!"

Keun Umma explained to me that in Korean culture, people often fought over who should pay for things.

"Everyone is always too polite to let the other person pay, especially when it comes to family," she said. "You should see the tricks Keun Appa plays to get the bill at family dinners!"

I laughed. Keun Appa was nice, and he was funny, too!

The outdoor market was really busy, with shops selling everything from clothes to yummy snacks and pretty fans. Above our heads, there were small flags from countless countries hanging from strings. I spotted the American flag right next to the Korean one!

"The flags are there to help visitors feel welcome. This is a popular tourist area for people from all over the world," explained Dad.

When I looked more closely at the crowds, I realized Dad was right! People from many different countries walked around the market and spoke in all sorts of languages. It was almost like being back in California!

The first shop that caught my eye was a booth selling lots of cute, bright clothes. The T-shirts had really adorable animals with happy smiles on them, and I really wanted one!

"Again, get whatever you want, Mindy," Grandpa said with a big smile. "Your harabeoji has been waiting to spoil you on this trip!"

I giggled. "Okay!"

I was so tempted to get a shirt with a dog or a cat on it, but I already had lots of shirts like that. I wanted to get something that would remind me of Korea.

The travel guidebook I'd read yesterday had said that the national animal of South Korea was the tiger. When Korea hosted the Olympics a long time ago, the mascot was a cartoon tiger!

I spotted a bright yellow shirt with a dancing tiger on the front. It looked so happy and made me happy too!

"Can I have this shirt, Harabeoji?" I asked.

Grandpa took the shirt from me. "How cute! Great choice. I'd be happy to buy this for you."

"Yay!" I cheered. "Gomap seum-nida!"

*Gomap seum-nida* means "thank you" in Korean!

Keun Appa bought Sora and Sung-jin shirts too. Sora got a pink shirt with a dog that looked like Danbi the Pomeranian, while Sung-jin got a blue shirt with a penguin. All our shirts were amazing!

A few blocks later, I saw a store selling bags shaped like various cartoon characters and friendly-looking animals. The one that caught my eye was teal blue and shaped like a smiling bear.

"That bag is so cute!" I said.

Grandpa snatched it from the rack, sounding triumphant as he said, "I'll buy you this, too!"

"I can get it!" exclaimed Dad.

Dad and Grandpa argued some more about who should buy me the bag, but Grandpa won again. Everyone laughed.

"Gomap seum-nida!" I said again.

Even though I appreciated that Grandpa was buying me stuff, I did feel bad. I didn't want him to go bankrupt! At another store full of souvenirs, I decided to get one last thing: a small, pocket-sized Korean flag that I could take back home.

When I handed the flag to him, Grandpa laid it out on his hands. His eyes got all shiny, just like Dad's do when he is about to cry. "Is this what you want, Min-jung?" he asked.

"Yup, I want something to remember Korea by!"

Grandpa looked so proud of me. Everyone did!

After we were done shopping, we grabbed lunch from the street-food vendors. Everyone got really yummy food like tteokbokki, dumplings, and knife-cut noodle soup. Julie got kimbap rolls, like the ones she was planning to make!

Kimbap is like sushi, except instead of fish, it has beef, eggs, and lots of other yummy things in it. Julie closely looked at the kimbap, like she was trying to remember all the ingredients.

When no one else was looking, I gave her a thumbs-up. I hoped she'd be able to make the kimbap successfully!

After we were done with lunch, we left the market and headed to our next destination. We were on a fun city adventure!

# Chapter 7

Our next stop was Gyeongbokgung, the Korean royal palace. It's where the king and queen used to live back when Korea still had a royal family!

Gyeongbokgung was built a long time ago, but it's surrounded by tall skyscrapers and modern museum buildings. I thought it was really cool how Seoul was a mix of the old and new.

People from all over the world were wearing hanbok, traditional Korean clothes, as they walked around the palace grounds. Everyone looked so pretty!

Dad got out his phone and selfie stick from his bag and handed them to me.

"Here," he said. "How would you like to be the family photographer for today?"

I grinned. I'd never used a selfie stick before, but I was so excited to try it out!

"I can take pictures too!" Sung-jin said. He got his own selfie stick from his bag, and soon he and I were running around taking pictures of everything. It was so much fun!

Tour groups speaking many different languages walked around the palace grounds. We didn't need a tour guide, though. We had Grandpa! He knew everything from how the king held court to what happened to the royal family in the end. Dad translated in English when Grandpa said words I didn't know. Grandpa and Dad were both so smart!

I also took a lot of pictures with Grandpa and Grandma all over the palace. There were so many pretty locations, like the wide courtyard and the queen's quarters. I also took lots of fun group photos with Julie and the entire family.

Dad promised he'd send the pictures to my grandparents, so they'd have them too. "That way,

even when we are an entire ocean and continent apart, we can all remember the time we spent together," Dad said.

When we were leaving the palace, I saw some kids my age wearing hanbok. It reminded me of *my* own hanbok back home. It was my favorite because Mom had bought it for me a long time ago, but now it was too small for me. I couldn't get a new one back home in Florida because there weren't any hanbok stores there.

Dad saw where I was looking.

"Hey, Mindy, since we're in Seoul, why don't we stop by a store and get you measured for a new hanbok?" Dad asked. "They can probably send it to Keun Appa's apartment once it's done, and he can send it to us in Florida."

"I sure can!" Keun Appa said. "Just give the shop my phone number and address."

"Wow, thanks, Keun Appa! That's so nice of you." I got really excited. Finally, I could get a new hanbok! And it would be extra special since it was from Korea.

Because Grandma and Grandpa were tired from all the walking around, my cousins' family went to a café with them while Julie, Dad, and I walked to the nearest hanbok store. It had hanbok in lots of different colors, like yellow, pink, blue, and green.

A nice lady measured my arms, my neck, and other areas. I got to choose the fabric and designs, too. I felt like I was getting fitted for my own princess gown!

The lady said that my hanbok would be ready in a month, but I could try on a similar, already made one now so I could see what it'd look like.

I picked a hanbok with the same colors as the one I ordered: a light yellow top and a red skirt. It was really different from the pink-and-rainbow one Mom had bought me a long time ago, but it was still cute.

When I tried it on, Dad gasped. "Mindy, you look so grown-up!"

His eyes were shiny. He seemed so proud.

I stared at myself in the mirror. Unlike the old hanbok, this hanbok was my size. And Dad was right. I did look more grown-up! And I looked like I belonged in Korea.

On the way back home, Julie and I told Dad about Julie's plan to make kimbap. My grandparents were napping in their seats, but we talked in English just in case, so it wouldn't ruin Julie's surprise.

"You really don't have to make anything," Dad said, "but that's so sweet of you. We're going camping tomorrow, so kimbap will be the perfect snack. If you want me to, I'll do my best to help!"

"Me too!" I said, raising my hand. "I volunteer!"

Julie smiled. "Aw, thanks, you two! Brian, could you take your parents out for tea tomorrow morning? I'm sure they'd love spending some alone time with you, and it'll give me time to make things."

"Got it," Dad said. "I can definitely do that."

"And, Mindy," continued Julie, "can you come to the grocery store with me and help me get all the ingredients? I don't know much Korean, so I'd appreciate the help."

"Sure!" I said. "I'm not good at reading and writing in Korean, but I'll try my best!"

"Your Korean is still better than mine," Julie said with a laugh. "With our Korean skills combined and the Internet, I'm sure we can figure everything out!"

I was so excited for what we had planned tomorrow. I felt like a secret agent about to carry out an important mission!

# Chapter 8

Julie and I went to the Korean grocery store first thing in the morning. Before we left, I thought about asking Sora or Sung-jin for help but decided not to. I didn't want to look silly when I didn't know a lot of the words! Plus, they were still sleeping when we left.

When we got to the store, though, I knew we were in trouble! Unlike back home in Florida, there wasn't any English on the signs, so it was really confusing. I tried my best to understand the Korean signs and labels, but Julie and I still ended up walking in circles to try to find everything. By the time we were done shopping, I was pretty dizzy.

Keun Appa and Keun Umma were busy preparing for our camping trip when we got back home.

"Feel free to use the kitchen!" Keun Umma said with a smile.

"Byung-hoon told us about your plans," Keun Appa explained, using Dad's Korean name, "so we got the other food ready first."

"Thank you so much!" said Julie.

The first part of making kimbap requires lots of cooking and cutting, so Julie said I couldn't help out with that. "If you want, you can help put all the ingredients together later, though," she said.

"Okay!" I said.

I went to go update my blog. For today's entry, I wrote about my trip to Seoul and included lots of pictures of my family and me. Just looking back at the photos made me so happy!

When I was done, I went back to the kitchen. The room smelled like freshly cooked meat and sesame oil. All the different vegetables and other kimbap ingredients were neatly laid out on the table.

"Perfect timing!" Julie said. "I was just about to

put the ingredients together in the rolls. Let's try making only one first so we can taste it before we make the rest."

"Okay!"

Julie spread rice onto the dried seaweed, and I put strips of beef, egg, carrot, spinach, and pickled radish on the rice. It reminded me of how when I was little, I used to help Mom make kimbap too.

Julie used a bamboo mat to roll up the kimbap and then cut it into bite-sized pieces with a knife. It looked so good!

"Yay!" I said when the kimbap was ready to eat. "Let's try it!"

Julie took one kimbap piece, and I grabbed another. We put the kimbap in our mouths.

It *looked* like the kimbap Mom used to make, but the taste was different. Instead of being a mix of sweet and savory, it was just really sweet! *Too* sweet!

I didn't want to hurt Julie's feelings, so I didn't say anything.

play in, so lots of kids go mulnori there!"

rive to Gangwon-do was almost three

t it was worth it, because Gangwon-do

etty! The mountains were green, and the

d rivers were so shiny and clear. Lots of

ilies were playing in the water or setting

lready.

we found an empty area by a creek, Dad

Appa set up a tent with some lawn chairs

ndparents could have somewhere to rest

olayed.

, a lot of other kids were in the creek.

e either splashing around in the shal-

or floating on tubes and floaties in the

rts. It looked really fun!

ou to the water!" yelled Sung-jin.

Keun Umma said. "Everyone needs to

nscreen before you get in the water. And

ed to inflate the tubes!"

d Julie helped us apply sunscreen while

a and Dad inflated our floaties. We had

shaped like a unicorn and another one

"Oh no!" Julie exclaimed. She spit out her piece. "This is definitely not right!"

Sora and Sung-jin came out of their rooms then. They'd changed out of their pajamas and were wearing T-shirts and shorts.

"I want to try!" Sora said.

Before anyone could stop her, she took a kimbap from the plate and put it in her mouth.

"Ew!" Sora exclaimed, making a face. "It's so sweet!"

Julie frowned. "I wonder what went wrong. Maybe I didn't add enough salt?"

She grabbed the bag of salt from the counter. When they saw the bag, Sung-jin and Sora giggled.

"That's not salt! That's sugar!" Sung-jin said. "See? It says seol-tang. That's sugar! Salt is so-geum."

He pointed at the bag, and I looked more closely at the letters and gasped. I'd made a horrible mistake!

"Ohhhh!" I cried out. "Oh no!"

"What happened?" Ju

"I got salt and sugar
only remembered that th
with an *s* and had two
messed up."

Instead of being mad,

"It's okay, Mindy," sh
made one roll. I can jus
that needed salt in them!

I felt really bad, but I w
my mistake was funny.

By the time Julie fini
bap, Dad came back with
all leave for Gangwon-do
camping trip!

"Gangwon-do is an ar
of mountains, rivers, and
vacation spot," Dad expl
place for mulnori!"

"What's mulnori?" I wa

"*Mulnori* is the Korea
water. Gangwon-do has a

are safe

The
hours. B
was so p
creeks a
other fa
up tents

Whe
and Keu
so my g
while w

Near
They w
low wa
deeper

"Ra

"Wa
put on
we still

She
Keun A
two: o

shaped like a watermelon. We also had a tube shaped like a pink donut for Sora. Everything was so cute!

After we were done putting on sunscreen, Sung-jin and I helped by laying out a dotjari in front of the tent. A dotjari is a large plastic fold-able mat that can be used for a picnic.

And then it was finally time for mulnori!

# Chapter 9

"Ya-ho!" yelled Sung-jin as he ran to the water. It's how Korean kids say "Yippee!"

Sora and I followed him. Sung-jin and I were carrying the big floaties, while Sora had the pink donut around her waist.

"Stay in the shallow area for a bit before you venture farther!" Dad reminded us.

"Okay!" I replied as we splashed into the shallow area.

The water was cold and felt really nice in the summer heat. It was so clear that I could see the pebbles on the bottom.

A great big splash hit my face.

"Hey!" I cried out.

Sung-jin gave me a big grin. "You can splash me back! Let's have a splashing fight!"

I did what he said, and we laughed. Sora joined in too, and soon all three of us were soaking wet.

When we got bored of splashing, we pulled our floaties into the deeper water and swam around with the other kids. Mulnori was the perfect summer activity!

After a while, though, I got hungry. Yummy smells of Korean barbecue drifted to where we were playing in the water.

"Lunchtime!" said Dad.

Keun Appa was grilling barbecue on the portable stove while the other adults laid out Korean pancakes, kimchi, and Julie's kimbap, picnic-style, on the dotjari. Sung-jin, Sora, and I changed into dry clothes and helped too, laying out plates and chopsticks for everyone. And then we all started eating!

The barbecue grilled by Keun Appa was good, but so was Julie's kimbap. It was so much better with all the right ingredients!

"This is amazing!" Dad said as he ate one of the pieces. He gave Julie a hug. "Good job."

My grandparents tried the kimbap too.

"This is wonderful!" Grandma said. "You did great."

She smiled at Julie, and Julie looked really happy when Dad translated what she said.

While we were eating, Sora told everyone about how bad the kimbap had tasted when Julie first made it.

"They thought sugar was salt!" she said. "So funny!"

Everyone laughed, even my grandparents. I blushed.

"I guess, next time I shouldn't be afraid to ask for help," I said.

"Yup, there's no shame in not knowing something, Mindy," Dad said. "And I'm sure your cousins will be more than happy to help you!"

"Yeah!" Sung-jin said. "It's okay. I'm not very good at reading English, so we're even."

"I can help too!" Sora said. "Don't forget about me!"

Everyone laughed again. Sora was so cute!

After we ate, we played some more until it started to get dark. Keun Umma turned on our lamps and we sat around in a circle on the dotjari. Dad made us cup ramen noodles using the portable stove, and we ate them with kimchi. It was simple, but it was the perfect dinner for a camping trip!

Keun Appa got out his guitar and sang us old Korean songs. Dad and Grandpa sang along too.

This was my first time hearing Dad sing in Korean! Julie and I cheered extra hard for Dad.

Suddenly, Sora gasped and pointed at the woods near our tent.

"Look," she said. "Fireflies!"

I'd never seen fireflies before, and I loved how small and bright they were. Their golden lights blinked on and off as they floated around. It was almost like they were dancing to the music!

Afterward, we spread out on the dotjari and looked up at the night sky. We could see so many stars from here, and the crescent moon was bright.

"Mindy," Dad whispered. "Isn't it really cool how, even though we're now in Korea, we can still see the same moon as the one that's visible in Florida?"

"Yeah," I said. "It makes the world seem a lot smaller!"

I was going to miss my family so much when we went back to America, but it made me feel better that no matter where I was, we'd always be looking at the same moon.

# Chapter 10

All too soon, it was our last night in Korea. We'd only been here for two weeks, but I felt like I was going back home as a brand-new person! I'd eaten so many new foods, learned so many things about Korean culture, and bought lots of cute stuff. I'd also studied Korean a lot too!

Julie tried making food again, but this time, everyone helped out. Keun Umma and my cousins helped Julie and me get all the ingredients at the grocery store, and Grandma cooked with Julie. It was a family team effort!

Watching Julie and Grandma preparing food together made me really happy. Even though they couldn't understand each other through words, they were able to communicate through smiles and food. Together they made so many yummy things, like japchae, bulgogi, and dumplings. I helped when I could too.

By the time we were done, my stomach was growling a lot. Everything smelled so good!

The whole family sat down for our last family dinner. While we ate, Grandma and Grandpa gave a speech in Korean! Dad translated in English so Julie and I could understand everything.

"We were really sad to lose Hee-jung," Grandpa said, using Mom's Korean name. "She was such a good wife and mother, and we all loved her so much. We were afraid our son wouldn't be happy again. But then he met Julie, and it's been so nice to see him smile."

"Welcome to the family, Julie," added Grandma. "Thank you for everything you do for our son."

Everyone at the table had happy tears, and Dad hugged Julie real tight.

\* \* \*

The next day, we were done loading our suitcases into Dad's rental car when Grandpa said, "Min-jung, can Halmeoni and I speak to you in the living room?"

I looked to Dad, but he shrugged. "You should go ahead and see what your grandparents want to say to you, Mindy. We still have time."

In the living room, my grandparents were sitting on the floor cushions. They had serious looks on their faces. I hoped they weren't mad at me!

I sat down on the cushion in front of them.

Grandpa didn't smile at me when I sat. He looked kind of scary!

"Min-jung, since this is your last day in Korea, your halmeoni and I wanted to talk to you, just the three of us."

"Sure, Harabeoji, what is it?" I asked.

"We don't get to see you often like we get to see Sora and Sung-jin, so we wanted to give you some words of wisdom before you left. Grandparents in Korea give their grandchildren advice all the time if they live close to each other, but since you live so far away . . . I hope this advice will help you in the next school year."

"First of all," Grandma said, "be nice to everyone, even when they are not nice to you. You never know who will end up being your friend, and it's good to have as many friends as you can."

"And listen to your dad and other adults," added Grandpa. "But also, don't be afraid to do what you think is right. You're a smart girl, Min-jung. Don't forget that!"

"Last but not least," said Grandma, "believe in yourself and your ability to achieve your dreams. You have a bright future ahead of you, and you will be a great person one day."

When Grandma finished, Grandpa reached behind him and got out a thick white envelope. He handed it to me with a sly smile.

"Don't tell your dad we gave you this, okay?" he said. "It's a special, secret gift from us to you."

I looked into the envelope.

"Wow," I said. "That's a lot of American money!"

"Your harabeoji and I went to the bank to

convert the money so you can spend it with your friends back home," Grandma explained.

"Wow! Thanks, Halmeoni! Thanks, Harabeoji!" I exclaimed.

We all went in for a big group hug. I felt so safe and warm in my grandparents' arms. I wished I could hug them forever.

I started crying. I was going to miss them so much!

"Don't cry, Mindy," said Grandpa. "Remember, we're always only a phone call away."

"And," Grandma added with a grin, "I have a feeling we'll see each other again very soon."

She glanced back at where Dad and Julie were laughing together by the door and gave me a big wink.

# Chapter 11

When it was time for us to leave, the entire family came down to the parking lot to say good-bye.

"Hope you had a good visit, Min-jung!" Keun Appa said.

"I did," I said. "Thanks so much for everything, Keun Appa!"

Dad, Julie, and I went around to say good-bye to everyone. Sora, Sung-jin, and I promised to keep in touch. They'd always been my cousins, but now they were also my friends! Before I got in the car, I hugged Grandma and Grandpa again one last time.

As we were driving away, I looked back and

saw my family waving at us. My grandparents were smiling, but they were also crying. I started crying again too! I really hoped I would see them again soon, just like Grandma said I would.

The drive to the airport seemed a lot slower than the one to my relatives' apartment, and so did the flight. Even though I knew we had to go back home, a large part of me didn't want to leave.

I fell asleep on the plane, and when I woke up, we were back in the United States! The trip to Korea seemed like a long, good dream.

When we landed back home in Florida, Dad's phone went off.

He checked it and smiled. "Aw, look at this, Mindy!"

He showed me his phone. It was a picture of Theodore and Oliver lying side by side with their tongues sticking out. Below it was a text from Eunice that said: **Waiting for you to come back home!**

I smiled for the first time since we left Korea. I

was still sad from leaving my family behind, but I was so excited to see Theodore again!

After we left the airport, we dropped Julie back at her house.

"Thanks for being my cooking partner in crime, Mindy," she said. Julie gave me a big hug before she got out of the car. "It was so special to be in Korea with you and your dad."

I smiled. I was really happy she came on the trip with us too!

And then, finally, it was time to pick up Theodore. When we arrived, I could hear Theodore and Oliver barking in the house.

"Welcome back!" Eunice said as she opened the door. Theodore ran straight to me and jumped up and down. I picked him up and he licked my face.

"I missed you so much, Theodore!" I said. "Did you have a good time with Oliver?"

Theodore wagged his tail. He couldn't talk, but he looked happy. And I was so glad to see him again!

When we got home, Dad unloaded our suitcases.

"We can unpack everything tomorrow," he said.
"Let's shower and go to bed!"

After sleeping on the floor for two weeks, I was
so happy to get into my own bed. It felt like I was
lying on a cloud! Theodore cuddled up next to me,
like he always did. I'd missed this so much!

Dad came into my room to tuck me in.

"Did you have a fun time, Mindy?" Dad asked.
"You can be honest, since it's just you and me."

"Yeah!" I said. "It wasn't fun at first, but I had a
really good time in the end. Everyone was so nice,
and we did so many cool things!"

Dad smiled. "That's good! I'm glad you liked it.
And I think your Korean improved so much as well."

"Yup!" I replied. "I became more of an expert!"

Dad laughed and kissed me good night.

After he left, I snuggled close to Theodore and
fell asleep, dreaming of walking around the royal
palace with my grandparents.

# Acknowledgments

It's somehow a brand-new year of Mindy Kim books, and as always, I have so many people that I'd like to thank. I wouldn't be the writer (or person, honestly!) I am today without my grandparents, who always supported my dreams and continually reminded me that I'd be "a great person one day." I get my love of books and storytelling from my grandparents, who always told me stories about their own lives and applauded my love for reading. Although most of them have passed away now, I will eternally be grateful for their love, which stretched for thousands of miles and consisted of

79

decades' worth of "Happy New Year" and "Happy Birthday" calls. I am also so grateful for the rest of my relatives in South Korea and for all that they did to make sure my parents and I had a great time whenever we visited from the States. This book wouldn't have been possible without all the memories my family and I made together.

I wrote the majority of this book while I was in the mandatory two-week quarantine in South Korea during the COVID-19 pandemic, and I probably couldn't have written it without the support of my friends and loved ones. Thank you to my parents, Aneeqah Naeem, Alice Zhu, Sarah Wu, Faridah Abike-Iyimide, Rey Noble, Katie Zhao, Kaiti Liu, Francesca Flores, Annie Lee, Angelica Tran, Brianna Lei, Amelie Zhao, Oanh Le, Victor Hu, Stephanie Lu, Bernice Yau, Chelsea Chang, Shiyun Sun, Luke Chou, Antony Rivera, and Sharon Choi for making this whole pandemic bearable. An extra shout-out goes to Antony for talking me through story ideas when I was stuck writing this book.

Thank you to all the readers, parents, teachers,

librarians, and booksellers who've continued to show their love and support for Mindy. Debuting as an author during a pandemic was definitely not ideal, but I am all the more grateful for the friends that Mindy was able to find, despite it all. And, as always, thank you to everyone who is involved in the making of this book. I know as well as anyone how challenging it can be to work during a pandemic, so I'm so appreciative of all the people who worked to bring Mindy's story to life during a global crisis. Here's hoping that things are better by the time this book comes out in 2021, and if not, it's my hope that, at the very least, this book brings joy to readers, if only for a short while.

# About the Author

Lyla Lee is the author of the Mindy Kim series as well as the YA novel *I'll Be the One*. Although she was born in a small town in South Korea, she's since then lived in various parts of the United States, including California, Florida, and Texas. Inspired by her English teacher, she started writing her own stories in fourth grade and finished her first novel at the age of fourteen. After working various jobs in Hollywood and studying psychology and cinematic arts at the University of Southern California, she now lives in Dallas, Texas. When she is not writing, she is teaching kids, petting cute dogs, and searching for the perfect bowl of shaved ice. You can visit her online at lylaleebooks.com.